D1262507

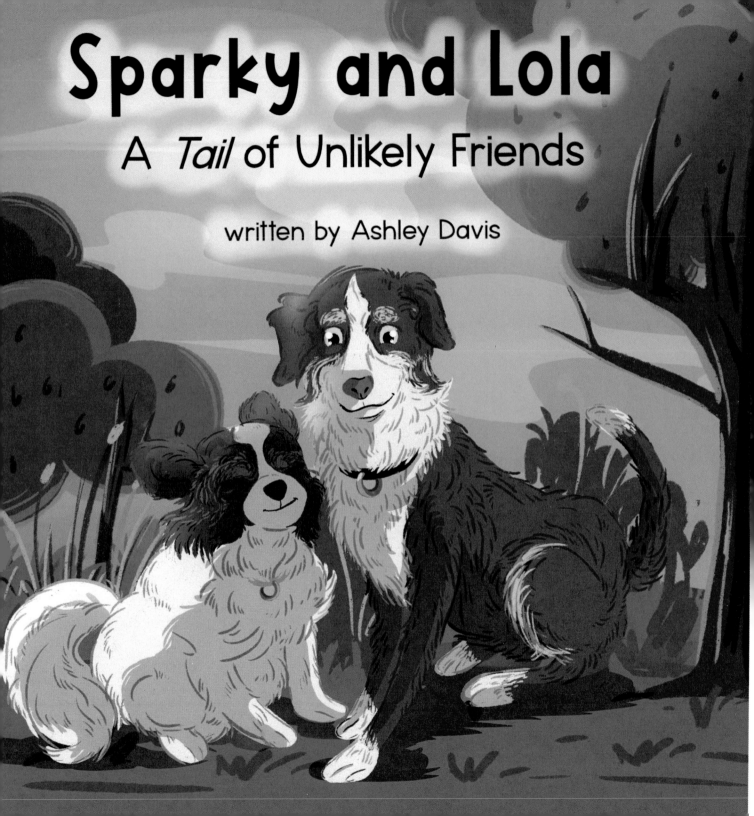

Sparky and Lola

A *Tail* of Unlikely Friends

written by Ashley Davis

To Gavin and Michael, with all my love.
And to Auntie Sue.-A.D.

For information contact:
Ashley E. Davis / Magic in Room 103 at www.magicinroom103.com

MAGIC IN ROOM 103

Written by Ashley Elizabeth Davis
Commercial Use Fonts by Kaitlynn Albani
Illustrated by Aaditya Singh

Library of Congress Registration Number / Date: TXu002302412 / February 07, 2022

First Edition: 2022

ISBN: 979-8-9867595-1-7 (eBook)
ISBN: 979-8-9867595-0-0 (Paperback)
ISBN: 979-8-9867595-2-4 (Hardcover)

The first time I saw Lola, I was curious!

She was a small dog, with brown eyes, big, pointy ears and the tiniest paws. Lola's tail was curled. Her hair was mostly white, and her tri-colored face markings made her small face look like she was wearing a mask.

Of course, I knew Lola was also a dog. Dogs notice these things! But she doesn't LOOK like ME, I thought to myself.

The first time our human Gavin walked us, Lola couldn't keep up!
I couldn't help but notice, she certainly had an interesting odor - if you know what I mean!
She doesn't SMELL like ME, I thought.

Lola loved to bark at the passing critters. Her voice reminded me of a song. But she doesn't SOUND like ME, I thought.

Time passed, and the leaves on the trees outside started to turn colors.

One autumn day, Lola was under the weather, so our humans took her to the veterinarian for a check-up. I waited restlessly at home

When they got home, Lola seemed glad to see me, too!

We may not be just alike, I realized, but we're both good dogs.
Lola has been my best pal ever since.

The first time I met Sparky, I was weary.

He was a medium - sized dog - no doubt still a puppy - with green eyes, floppy ears, and massive paws. Sparky's tail was long and straight, with a white patch of fur at the tip. His fur was mostly red, with spots of white, and copper markings that looked like eyebrows above his bright green eyes.

Naturally, I knew Sparky was also a dog. Dogs recognize these things! But he doesn't LOOK like ME, I thought to myself.

The first time Gavin walked both of us, Sparky destroyed my leisurely stroll! He would not slow down, and I wanted to stop and sniff my favorite tree. And pardon me – but his stench was too offensive to overlook! His AROMA is nothing like MINE, I noted.

Sparky howled at every bird we saw. His bark doesn't SOUND like MINE, I thought.

Time passed, and I knew I was stuck with him!

Then one day, I wasn't feeling well. Our humans took me to the veterinarian for a check-up. Turns out, I had a cold and the vet said I would feel better soon.

When I got home, Sparky was waiting
impatiently for me – and I found that I was
quite happy to see him.

We may have our differences, I realized, but we're both good dogs. Sparky has been my dearest friend ever since.

THE END

Ashley is a mom, wife, and teacher. Sparky and Lola: A Tail of Unlikely Friends is her first children's book. The characters are inspired by her son Gavin, her Papillion (Lola), and Australian Shepherd (Sparky). Teaching children to read is her passion, and books that lend themselves to teaching Point of View are her favorite! The story's message of acceptance is one she truly believes in. Ashley loves iced coffee, @ulu_leaf earrings, and rainy days. She lives in Rhode Island with her family.